4. A Ghost of a Chance

He and Anil passed the ball between themselves a few times while the mill children watched the demonstration in obedient silence. Ryan, however, soon lost his patience.

"They don't want a boring old coaching session from you, Worm. Let me show 'em how to score a goal. That's what football's all about."

The Rangers' top striker stepped in to intercept a pass and dribbled the ball away before lashing it against a wall. "GOAL!" he yelled at the top of his voice, punching the air in mock celebration. "GOAL!"

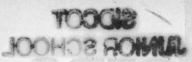

Also in this series:

Look out for:

TiME RANGERS

4. A Ghost of a Chance

Rob Childs

DAZZA
GOALKEEPER — 1

WORM
RIGHT-BACK — 2

STOPPER
CENTRE-BACK — 5

RAKESH
RIGHT-MIDFIELD — 4

MR STOPPARD
MANAGER

JACKO
CENTRE-MIDFIELD — 8

SPEEDIE
RIGHT-WINGER — 7

RYAN
CENTRE-FORWARD — 9

ANIL
LEFT-WINGER — 11

MR THOMAS
MANAGER

For my wife Joy, with special thanks

Scholastic Children's Books,
Commonwealth House, 1–19 New Oxford Street,
London WC1A 1NU, UK
a division of Scholastic Ltd
London ~ New York ~ Toronto ~ Sydney ~ Auckland

Published in the UK by Scholastic Ltd, 1997

Copyright © Rob Childs, 1997
Cover illustration copyright © Stuart Williams, 1997
Inside illustrations copyright © Kenny McKendry, 1997

ISBN 0 439 01127 5

Typeset by DP Photosetting, Aylesbury, Bucks.
Printed by Cox & Wyman Ltd, Reading, Berks.

10 8 6 4 2 3 5 7 9

1 Arrival

"Mine's a top bunk!" yelled Ryan as he bolted for the stairs.

Dazza was already halfway up them. "Slowcoach!" he jeered. "It's every man for himself."

"Hold on! Captain has first pick," Jacko called out in vain.

Worm's case suddenly burst open in the crush, spilling most of his dirty clothes down the steps. "I don't believe it!" he cried, scrambling back against the flow of traffic. "Save me a bed, some-body."

It was a forlorn hope. His plea went

unheard as the young footballers of Tanfield Rangers left no one in any doubt that they had arrived at the hostel. They clattered up the wooden stairway, shouting their rival claims for places in the two big dormitories on the second floor.

Ryan's dad, Mr Thomas, tore up his intended room plan and threw it away. "Waste of time that was," he grunted. "May as well let them get on with it now."

"Aye, they'll sort it out between themselves one way or another," agreed Mr Stoppard, his fellow manager. "Just glad we've got a separate room. Can you imagine having to share with that noisy lot?"

He noticed his own son helping Worm to gather up the scattered items. "And why didn't you join the stampede like all the other elephants?"

"No rush, Dad," Stopper grinned. "Sent my partner ahead to grab bunks by a window. I've got Speedie's case so it didn't slow him down."

"Good thinking," smiled his dad. "Speedie's well named. Saw him disappear up those stairs like a ferret up someone's trousers!"

The overnight stay in a hostel just outside Mannington marked the end of the Rangers' week-long Easter soccer tour of the Peak District. Their third and final match was the following day, Friday, against an under-twelve team from a local boarding school.

"Makes a nice change, this, from camping," said Rakesh, sprawled across his bottom bunk. "Hope they bang that tea-gong soon."

There was no response from the occupant of the sagging mattress above him. The temptation was too great to resist. Rakesh sat up and prodded the bulge through the springs with a handy football boot.

"Oi! Pack that in!" came the loud complaint. "I'll jump down and belt you if you do that again."

Rakesh giggled. "What's it like up there? Need an oxygen mask?"

"No thanks," retorted Dazza, leering down over the side of the bunk. "Just some peace from you. I'm knackered after that long hill-walk."

"You're always moaning. Thought you liked it in the hills."

"I did, but we've had no sleep for about two days, remember. Need to get all the rest I can now before tomorrow."

"Goalies don't need rest," Rakesh teased his pal. "It's us out on the pitch who do all the running about. You can just lean on the goalpost."

"Huh! Wish I could!" Dazza grunted. "No chance with a defence like ours. Have to keep on my toes, ready to cover for any mistakes."

"Hey! I heard that," said Stopper,

making his entrance at last with the two suitcases. He dumped them on the floor near the opposite window. "I'm the one round here who holds our defence together."

Dazza had no wish to pick an argument with his big centre-back. "Yeah, well, I wasn't referring to you, Stopper. I meant the others, like."

"Good job too," Stopper grinned, tossing his coat on to the bed above Speedie. "Guess this one's mine, is it? Well done for getting it. Thought you wanted a top bunk as well."

"I did," Speedie muttered, glancing over towards the captain. "Jacko pulled rank and turfed me off that one he's got now."

Stopper gazed out of the window at the bleak ruins of Mannington's old cotton spinning mill right next to the hostel. "Pity about the view."

"Oh, sorry," said Speedie sarcasti-

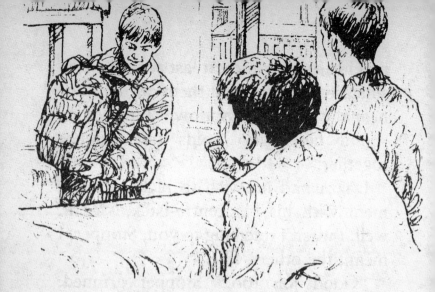

cally. "I'll go and change it for you, shall I? What would you like instead? Snow-capped mountains? A golden beach with dolphins leaping about the bay?"

"No, just a few trees to hide that old dump would do fine, thanks. Looks like a prison."

"It was in a way," said Worm, sorting out his belongings on the bunk beneath Jacko. "For the poor mill workers, that is. Kids younger than us, some of 'em, working all hours in there."

"That doesn't sound much fun," said Anil, Rangers' leggy left-winger, from across the other side of the room.

"Fun? Bet they didn't even know the meaning of the word," said Worm, inspecting his favourite T-shirt that somebody had trampled on. "It was all work and no play, six days a week."

"What about Sundays?"

"Don't encourage him, Anil," said Rakesh. "You know what Worm's like. If he thinks anybody's interested, he'll give us all a history lesson."

Worm chose to ignore the interruption. "They went to Sunday School, if they were lucky."

"*Lucky!* You call that lucky?" scoffed Ryan, dribbling a ball between the sets of bunks. "What about playing football in the afternoon like us?"

"You must be joking. No games allowed on Sundays."

"Probably had no energy left, anyway,

after all that work," Dazza chipped in. "Just like me at the minute."

"You don't know you're born, compared to what life was like for them," Worm told him indignantly. "You must have learnt something at school about little kids slaving away in factories and mines two hundred years ago."

"I told you," groaned Rakesh. "Shut him up, somebody, will you!"

"Goal!" cried Ryan suddenly. His shot had slammed against the door and rebounded back at even greater pace, just missing Speedie's head.

"Watch it!"

"Won't hurt you," Ryan laughed. "It's dead light, this ball."

"I'll bust it, if it comes near me again."

Ryan laughed even more. "I'd like to see you try. It's the world's first indestructible ball!"

"What are *you* doing with it, then?"

sneered Speedie. "You lot have already lost three leather ones this week."

Speedie was the only boy in their eight-berth dormitory who needed to ask that question. The others knew exactly where the ball had come from. They had all done far more travelling in the last few days than was scheduled on their tour itinerary – travelling backwards and forwards through time!

"Um, we're sort of testing it," Ryan stalled, searching for an answer. "It's the ball of the future!"

2 "Knackered"

"D'yer reckon this place is haunted?" said Rakesh, taking a break from the evening kickabout outside the hostel. "Must be dead ancient."

"Doesn't mean to say it has to be haunted," Anil replied.

"No, but in stories, old houses like this always have ghosts."

"Well, yeah, in stories maybe. Depends if you believe in such things."

Rakesh shrugged and then giggled. "Might be a laugh to see who does. How about trying to spook the others a bit tonight, eh?"

"Dunno. I think we could all do with a good night's sleep."

"C'mon, we want to have some fun while we're here, don't we?" Rakesh urged. "Let's go and have a quick look round to find a few props."

Anil trailed after him, leaving their mates playing with the bouncy ball in the open space between the mill and the hostel. A heavy tea was having its effects on the level of performance.

"C'mon, Jacko!" cried Speedie. "You should've got that pass easy."

Jacko didn't bother to chase the ball. "Too tired and too full. Early night for me, I've decided. Need to catch up on some sleep."

"What's the matter with you? Ryan's snoring been keeping you awake in the tent or something?"

"Or something," Jacko repeated vaguely.

Speedie looked at him. "Has something been going on this week that I don't know about?" he said accusingly. "Some people have been acting mighty strange at times on this tour. In fact, come to think of it, it's all you lot in our dorm – apart from me! What's the big secret?"

Jacko shook his head. "Soz. Can't say – not just yet. You wouldn't believe it, anyway. Still doesn't make much sense to me."

Worm hadn't joined in the kickabout. He was too busy nosing around the perimeter of the ruined cotton mill opposite the hostel. The three-storey brick building was in a sorry state. Shards of glass stuck out from its rotten window frames and the roof was littered with broken tiles. A metal fence prevented people from approaching too close.

He was disappointed at not being able to take a peep inside. Even if he risked squeezing through a gap in the fencing, the first row of windows was too high off the ground and the entrances were boarded up.

Worm gazed wistfully up in the gloom at the cracked, empty bell tower and tried to picture the mill as it might have looked in its prime. Apart from the skeletal remains of the giant water-wheel that once generated all the power, it reminded him of Tanfield's late-Victorian primary school.

"Forget it!"

Worm jumped, taken by surprise. "Oh, hi, Stopper! Er, just thinking."

"I can guess what you're thinking all right – so don't," Stopper grinned. "I know this time-travel business has been pretty amazing, but enough's enough. Give it a rest now, eh?"

"It's got nothing to do with me," Worm protested. "I'm not causing it – at least not deliberately. It just keeps happening."

"That's why it's best not to give it another chance. Stay away from old places like this, just in case."

Worm smiled sheepishly. "Be interesting, though, wouldn't it? Just imagine if we—"

"No!" Stopper said firmly. "C'mon, let's go back inside the hostel."

They turned away just as the football ballooned up and disappeared through one of the gaping windows to cries of dismay.

"That's it. End of game!" announced Jacko.

"End of ball too," Worm called out. "There's no way in, I've checked."

"There's got to be," insisted Ryan. "We'll break in and get it back in the morning when we can see what we're doing."

"It'll be too dangerous to go in there," Stopper told him sensibly. "Probably rat-infested too."

"Who cares about a few rats?" scoffed Ryan. "You don't have to come if you're scared."

Stopper didn't rise to the bait. He simply brushed past Ryan and marched back to the hostel. Before following him in, Worm took a last, lingering look at the desolate mill. "Thanks, ball," he whispered. "You've answered my prayers!"

The boys were met in the foyer by Mr Stoppard. "Shame you've lost that funny ball of yours," he said. "It seemed strangely familiar to me, somehow, but I can't quite place where I might have seen it before."

Even stranger to both managers was the fact that so many of the lads were only too happy to go upstairs to their dormitories. When Mr Thomas wandered into Ryan's room, he found his son and some of the others already in their sleeping bags.

"I'm wondering why you lot are all so suspiciously quiet," he said. "You're making me nervous. What are you planning?"

"Nothing, Dad," Ryan assured him. "Just saving our energy for the match tomorrow afternoon."

Mr Stoppard poked his head round the door too. "Thought this must be the wrong room, it's so peaceful."

"Probably got their bunks stuffed with goodies for a big midnight feast," said Mr Thomas. "Is that what it is, Dazza?"

The goalkeeper was a picture of innocence. "Come and search if you want. Once my head hits the pillow, I won't know a thing till morning."

"They're up to something, I can tell," remarked Mr Stoppard out in the corridor. "It's the lull before the storm."

Mr Thomas nodded thoughtfully. "This may be just a shot in the dark," he began, using his favourite expression, "but I think I know the reason. We'd better be doubly on our guard."

"What do you mean?"

"I've just realized tomorrow's date. It's April Fool's Day!"

When the men had gone, Speedie gazed around at his room-mates. "What is it with you guys? I thought we were gonna have loads of laughs tonight. Y'know, pillow fights and stuff and raiding the other dormitory."

"Another time," yawned Stopper. "We're all done in."

"Huh! Wish I'd gone next door now. I overheard them planning to stay awake telling jokes and messing about."

"If they keep us awake as well, we might go raiding after all," said Ryan threateningly. "Only it won't be in fun. We'll kill 'em!"

"It's OK. I've already warned them about making too much noise," said

Jacko. "There'll be no banging on walls or anything."

"I shouldn't bet on that, if I were him," hissed Rakesh to Anil across the gap between the bunks.

"Sshh, he'll hear us," whispered Anil, stifling his giggles.

"He'll hear us later on all right," Rakesh chuckled. "We'll make sure of that!"

3 Bumps in the night

"What was that?" Speedie sat up in bed and looked around him with bleary eyes. The others appeared to be fast asleep.

"Must have been dreaming," he murmured, then the noises came again – strange rattling and knocking sounds outside the dormitory.

"Who ... who's there?" he called out hesitantly.

Two knocks and a rattle answered his question.

"Stopper!" he hissed into the darkness. "Stopper! Wake up!"

No response, apart from a few sleepy grunts. Speedie listened to the rain lashing against the window pane, wondering what to do and fiddling with the zip on his sleeping bag. A sudden wail from the corridor made his mind up. He threw back the blanket cover, tumbled out of bed and began shaking the curled up lumps in the nearest bunks.

Worm just turned over and pulled the blanket back over his head.

"Uurgh! Gerroff!" Jacko slurred. "Wha's matter?"

"G – ghosts!" Speedie cried. "There's ghosts out there!"

"Don't talk stupid!" muttered Stopper. "If this is some crazy April Fool joke..."

"No joke, honest. Listen!"

Nothing. Stopper slumped back on to the pillow. "I'll murder you in the morning for this, Speedie," he promised.

"Don't go back to sleep," he pleaded.

"There's something out there, believe me. I've heard it."

"You've been having a nightmare," Jacko told him, raising himself up on one elbow. "Get back into bed."

A complaint came from across the room. "What's all the fuss about?"

"Soz, Dazza," Jacko apologized. "It's only Speedie cracking up. He reckons there's ghosts about."

"*Wwwhhhooooooooohhh!!*"

The terrible wail even woke Worm up. Jacko instinctively jumped down to the floor with a thump and then wished he hadn't. His top bunk suddenly seemed like a much safer place.

"What was that horrible noise?" Ryan grumbled, groggy with sleep.

The boys heard the chain-rattle for the first time, and there was more knocking on the wall. Then the door began to creak open. They all gaped at it, wide-eyed with fear. Something white appeared in the crack and Speedie couldn't choke down a squeal. He had been on edge for too long.

They watched as if in a trance, mesmerized by the creaking door and waiting for the next rattle or wail. A small white blob wobbled into the room, moaning.

"Where's Rakesh?" cried Worm. "And Anil?"

All eyes swivelled to the empty bottom bunks below Dazza and Ryan. "They've gone!" yelled Dazza. "They've been taken."

"No they haven't, you idiots!" Ryan hollered. Before anyone could stop him, he launched himself from his top bunk and flew across the room to attack the blob. It collapsed with a yelp underneath him.

"This is your ghost!" Ryan shouted in triumph. "Anil!"

The others joined in, whipping the

sheet off Anil's crumpled body and dragging Rakesh from the doorway, his length of chain clattering across the dormitory. Their pleas for mercy fell upon deaf ears.

"Right, you're both gonna get it now," Speedie threatened. "You scared the life out of us."

"Let's put 'em under the cold showers!" growled Dazza.

"Rather dangle them out of the window," said Ryan. "By their necks!"

"Quiet!"

The warning came from Worm, still lying in bed, and the others froze. The temperature in the room had suddenly dropped several degrees.

"It's happening..." Worm whispered. "Look!"

The grip on the captives' arms was relaxed as the boys stared about them. The room seemed to be shimmering, like a film going into a dream sequence.

For just a few seconds, the dormitory altered its appearance and gave them a fleeting glimpse of a quite different scene.

Dozens of small bodies littered the floor, huddled under blankets on thin mattresses, their heads covered by nightcaps. The boys' nostrils were assaulted by nauseating smells – a mixture of unwashed bodies, stale air and urine. Then the vision evaporated and they were surrounded again by the double bunks and their own strewn cases and sports bags.

"Wow!" breathed Rakesh, free now of any restraint. "Real ghosts!"

"Not ghosts," Worm murmured. "They were real kids, only from a long time ago. I think we've just had a little peep into the past."

"Reckon he's right," Stopper put in, standing by the curtainless window and peering through the rain. "That old mill

is up and working once more. There's light coming from every window."

They all dashed over to try and look. By the time Worm managed to squeeze his head through a gap, however, the view was fading and the mill returned to darkness.

"Will somebody please tell me what the hell is going on round here?" demanded Speedie. "I think I'm going mad!"

Speedie would not rest until the others let him into the secret of their previous time-travelling adventures. It was all too much to take in. Somehow, it seemed easier to believe in ghosts than what they told him about trips into the past and even the future.

His bewildered mind wrestled unsuccessfully with the problem. "But how come we saw what we did?"

They looked to Worm as usual for an explanation. He gave a little shrug.

"Maybe these kind of time-slips just happen occasionally. And after all our experiences, perhaps we've become sensitive to them."

"Something tells me this isn't all over yet either," said Stopper. "I can smell it."

"Yeah, what a pong!" grinned Rakesh.

"Sure was a bit crowded in here," said Anil, hoping his mates had at least forgiven him and Rakesh, even if they hadn't forgotten.

"And cold," nodded Dazza, giving a shudder.

"Those poor mill kids were probably used to it," said Worm. "I wonder if we were allowed to see them for a reason."

"He's off again," snorted Ryan. "He always says that."

"And I bet he'll want to find out what that reason is too," said Stopper with a heavy sigh.

4 Search party

"What a pathetic sight!" chuckled Mr Stoppard when the ghost-busting group trooped down late to breakfast. "Just look at 'em. Been up half the night, playing silly April Fool pranks on each other, I bet."

"Didn't you hear anything?" asked the pale-faced Speedie.

"Only the storm," said Mr Thomas. "Good job we weren't still in the tents. But you can expect a muddy pitch now for the game this afternoon."

"I'm looking forward to seeing the old boarding school again," said Mr Stoppard. "I was only there for a couple of years while my parents were working abroad, but I remember it had lovely big playing fields."

"They've done well to raise a team at Easter," Mr Thomas remarked. "Their lads are so soccer-mad, I gather they've even come back early from their holidays especially for this match."

"The school's very proud of its long footballing tradition. The game's been played there since the mid-nineteenth century."

"Bet their players are feeling a bit tired by now then!" Ryan laughed. "Wonder what the score is?"

"Cheeky monkey!" grinned Mr Stoppard. "I don't suppose any of you lazy lot want to come into town after breakfast? I've promised to take everyone else for a little stroll into Mannington to do some souvenir hunting."

Shopping was the last thing they felt

like doing. "Er, no, don't think so, Dad," replied Stopper. "We'd rather stay here and rest up a bit more."

"I'll see they don't get up to too much mischief," said Mr Thomas. "I need to check over the minibuses, anyway."

Back upstairs in the dormitory, the boys began to discuss their own plan of action for the morning.

"So what are we gonna do about that ball?" demanded Ryan.

"Nothing, if we've got any sense," replied Stopper.

"We can't just leave it there."

"We'll have to. Worm said there's no way into the mill."

"Um, actually, I think there may be a possible entrance," Worm murmured tentatively. They noticed a distinct gleam in his eye.

"I've just been reading this leaflet about the hostel," he explained. "Apparently, there's an underground passage linking it with the mill. Leads from the cellars. Might be worth checking out..."

He neglected to add that the hostel manager had told him the old tunnel collapsed long ago and had been bricked up. Worm wasn't interested in what it was like now. He hoped to find out how it used to be...

Half an hour later, the eight would-be explorers were standing around the outside entrance to the cellars at the rear of the hostel. They stared through the metal grille into the darkness below their feet.

"You got the torches out of the camping equipment, Ryan?" asked Jacko.

"Yeah, whipped them while Dad wasn't looking. He'd have only asked too many questions."

Jacko and Dazza hauled on the heavy

grille together. They lifted it slowly open on its rusty hinges until it leant back against the wall.

"I'm not so sure we should be doing this," said Anil. "I mean, we don't know what we're going to find down there."

"Our ball, with a bit of luck," grinned Ryan.

They shone the torches into the hole, relieved to see there was a chute and then only a short drop to the cellar's brick-lined floor.

"Right, then, who's first?" said Jacko.

Worm realized they were all looking at him. "Why is it always me?"

"You're the historian," said Ryan. "You're the one who most wants to try and see inside the mill."

"Yeah, but you're the one who keeps going on about this ball. Why don't *you* lead the way for a change?"

Ryan shrugged, peering again into the gloom. He swallowed hard. "OK, then. Suppose it'll be a dead end nowadays, anyway."

"Why do you reckon they had a tunnel?" asked Speedie.

"Maybe for taking supplies into the factory," Dazza suggested.

"And for carrying kids back out of sight when they got mangled up in the machinery," added Worm grimly.

Rakesh gave his ghostly chain a little clink. "We found this near here last night. Might come in useful again now."

He hooked the chain on to a metal bar and trailed the long loose end down the chute. "It'll help us to clamber back up later."

Ryan lowered himself on to the gently-sloping chute, gripping the sides as he eased his way downwards until his legs dangled over the drop. "Here goes," he said, stuffing the torch inside his top as he prepared to let go.

"Send us a postcard!" quipped Rakesh.

They saw Ryan land safely on all fours and then straighten up, pleased with himself. "Nothing to it," he called up.

"What's it like down there?" hissed Stopper.

"Damp and cold, but no sign of rats."

"Can you see any tunnel?" asked Worm.

"Not yet," came back the answer. "It's bigger than I thought. More than one room, by the look of it. I'll have to go and investigate."

"I'll come and join you," Worm called down. "No need for everyone to bother if it's just an empty cellar."

Worm held on to the chain and let gravity do most of the work, using the chute like a back-garden slide to slither down next to Ryan.

"You try that way and I'll go this," Worm said, indicating the directions with his torch beam. "Whistle if you see anything."

Their teammates waited impatiently above until a figure reappeared in their beams of light. "Any luck, Ryan?" asked Jacko.

"Nah. Pity. Looks like it's goodbye to the ball. Tell Worm I'll get him for leaving me down here on my own."

"What do you mean?" replied Jacko. "He's not come back out yet."

There was a moment's silence while Ryan considered the news. "Er, I'm not quite sure how to put this, guys," he faltered, "but I guess Worm must have gone and done another vanishing act!"

The footballers searched the cellars for Worm without success.

"A case for the X Files, this, I reckon!" grunted Rakesh.

"He can't be far away," said Jacko in exasperation, then checked himself. "Well, all right, he could be hundreds of years away, I know, but even so. He's got to be *somewhere*."

"Come and look at this part of the wall over here," Dazza called out. "See, the brickwork is lighter, as if it was done later. Perhaps this is where the tunnel was at one time."

"But that still doesn't explain where Worm's got to," sighed Anil and leant back against the wall. He suddenly disappeared from view. As he did so, a burst of noise reverberated into the cellars.

"What the...?" began Jacko.

"Where's he gone? He just fell straight through the wall!"

Rakesh whistled. "Wish he could've pulled off that trick last night!"

"This is crazy!" Ryan blurted out.

"No crazier than all the other ways we've found of travelling through time," Dazza shrugged. "This one must be a time tunnel!"

"That's impossible!" Speedie said, shaking his head in disbelief.

"We've just seen it can be done," said Dazza. He stretched out his left arm to feel the wall. Instead of meeting solid brick, his hand sank right through it. He stood there – handless – fighting the temptation to scream. Especially when he realized he couldn't pull his hand back.

"It was sucked in!" he exclaimed. "Sorry, I've got to go after it. I'm kind of attached to that hand. C'mon, follow me."

44

Dazza braced himself and slowly, bit by bit, eased the rest of his body through. The others hardly dared to watch, but the boy-eating wall in front of them demanded their full, stomach-churning attention.

"And then there were five..." murmured Rakesh.

"This is like some science-fiction/horror video," gulped Stopper. "I don't think I could stand watching anybody else get swallowed up like that. If we have to do it, we do it together, right?"

"I reckon this is something better done fast as well," said Rakesh. "Y'know, like pulling off a plaster. Quick wince rather than slow agony."

"OK, we'll hold hands and take a run at it," Jacko decided.

"No way!" stated Speedie flatly. "Sorry, captain, I'm not gonna run through a brick wall for anybody."

"Let's form a rugby scrum and barge

our way through," Ryan suggested.

"Not head first," stressed Speedie.

"Backwards, then," said Ryan. "I'm not fussy. C'mon, close up round me. Grab a hold."

They formed a clumsy, huddled scrum and manoeuvred into position, backs to the wall. "Right, ready?" Ryan cried. "Go!"

They shot backwards as if pushed by the All Blacks, collapsing in a heap in a candlelit tunnel which echoed to the sounds of clanking machinery.

"Hi, there!" Worm greeted them. "What kept you?"

5 Finders Keepers

"What's making all that racket?" Jacko grimaced.

"Spinning machines," answered Worm. "I nipped along to the end of the tunnel to have a quick peep in the mill. It's mind-boggling!"

"What time is it?" asked Anil. "And I don't mean ten o'clock!"

"Hard to say," Worm mused. "Industrial Revolution – late-eighteenth, early-nineteenth century, maybe even into Victorian times."

"Well, now we're here, we may as well all go and see what it was really like in those days," decided Dazza. "Better than just reading about it."

"Why don't we return to the cellar and climb outside again before it's too late?" put in Speedie nervously.

"'Fraid it already is," Dazza told him. "Time travel doesn't seem to work like that. It won't let us back to our own time till it's ready to."

"You'll get used to it," Worm said kindly.

"Doubt it. I still think this is some kind of bad dream I'm having. You're all just in my head."

"Thought it was a bit hot and stuffy," Rakesh remarked.

"You wait till you get inside the factory," said Worm ominously.

The noise from the rhythmic, clanking machines was almost unbearable, and the dust made the travellers choke as soon as they emerged from the tunnel. It also came as a shock to see children –

girls as well as boys – no older than themselves, and some looking even younger, hard at work amongst all the machinery and on the filthy floor.

There were men and women toiling at the machines, too, and although the eight newcomers were observed, nobody spoke to them. The workers glanced away if any of the strangers caught their eye.

"I can't stand much more of this!" shouted Jacko, straining to make himself heard above the clattering din. "Let's get outside."

As he spoke, he felt his tracksuit sleeve being tugged. He looked down and saw a boy kneeling under a workbench, his thin face staring up from beneath a cloth cap. The little lad said something, but Jacko couldn't pick up his words. The captain bent down as his teammates looked on.

"What did he want?" yelled Worm as Jacko straightened up again.

"He asked if we were the visitors. I didn't know what he meant so I just said yes."

This time it was Ryan who tugged at Jacko's clothing to get his attention. He pointed to something next to the bench. It was their ball.

A loud bell sounded at that moment and the boy snatched up the ball and shot away through the maze of machines before they could do anything. Children began to scuttle from every nook and cranny of the factory floor like beetles from under a stone. They were all heading for a doorway.

"Might as well follow them," shouted Worm. "Got to be something good."

It was. Fresh air. The young ragamuffins poured out into the cluttered backyard of the mill. Most of them immediately found a wall to sit or lean against to rest, but some started to play quiet little games.

The Rangers stumbled out into the yard just as the bell on the roof stopped its clanging. The noise of the spinning machines still came through the open windows, but at least the footballers could now hear themselves think. They blinked at the sight of so many scrawny children in such tattered, ill-fitting clothes and caps.

"There must be over a hundred of 'em," gasped Stopper.

"Pauper kids, mostly," said Worm. "Orphans – or from families that were too poor to look after them, and they got sent away to work here."

The Rangers themselves gradually became a major source of curiosity. Some of the mill children plucked up the courage to come nearer, if only to stare at their strange clothes, a mix of soccer kit, jeans and coats.

One of them was the skinny urchin with the ball. "What's your name?" asked Worm, hoping to sound friendly.

"Whizzer, Mister."

"Mister!" chuckled Anil.

"We probably do look like grown-ups to them," said Stopper.

"Right, Whizzer. I'm Worm ... I mean, Michael," he corrected himself as he saw the lad begin to smirk. "Why aren't you all busy working?"

"The Master's good to us," said Whizzer. "He gives us some free time once a week. The Master said we could play with some visitors today."

"Er, I don't think he meant us," said Jacko, shooting a glance at Worm. "We didn't know we were coming here ourselves till this morning."

"Look what I've got," Whizzer said, unconcerned about such details.

"Yes, it's our ball," Ryan butted in.

Whizzer's face fell. "What he means," said Worm quickly, "is that the ball is our present to you."

Worm ignored Ryan's protests. "We'll

show you a good game with it, shall we?" Worm offered, taking the ball gently out of Whizzer's hands and putting it on the ground. "Now watch, everyone. You use the side of your foot like this to kick the ball to your partner."

He and Anil passed the ball between themselves a few times while the mill children watched the demonstration in obedient silence. Ryan, however, soon lost his patience.

"They don't want a boring old coaching session from you, Worm. Let me show 'em how to score a goal. That's what football's all about."

The Rangers' top striker stepped in to intercept a pass and dribbled the ball away before lashing it against a wall. "GOAL!" he yelled at the top of his voice, punching the air in mock celebration. "GOAL!"

All the children laughed and Whizzer was the first to react. He ran after the rebound, controlled the awkward bounce with remarkable ease and then copied Ryan's shot. The ball flew into the wall, not as powerfully as Ryan's effort but almost in the same place, just missing a girl's head.

"GOAL!" he squealed, imitating Ryan's antics by jumping up and down and waving his fists about. "GOAL!"

The footballers applauded. "I think he's got the general idea, don't you?" grinned Jacko. "Anybody fancy a quick game?"

The next quarter of an hour was a gloriously mad free-for-all, during which any likeness to the modern game of football was purely coincidental. The Rangers kept urging that the ball should only be kicked and not handled, but at times the only thing that wasn't being kicked was the ball itself. Other people's shins were the favourite alternative.

Many girls joined the frenetic action,

too, and the numbers involved con-
stantly changed. Players kept dropping
out through exhaustion and then
charged back into the fray when they'd
recovered their breath.

"Which side are we supposed to be
on?" laughed Anil.

Dazza shrugged. "Just do what all this
lot are doing. If the ball comes near you,
bash it the way you're facing and run
after it."

Whizzer, though, was a natural foot-
baller. He and the ball went together like
jelly and ice-cream, even though he'd
never tasted either. They were made for
each other. When he was in possession,
the ball seemed to be an extension of his
own thin legs, like a balloon on a stick,
and he only lost it through being
crowded out or tripped over.

Or by scoring. The walls at each end of
the yard acted as targets and it was
usually Whizzer's black, scuffed boots

that slapped the ball against the brick-work. The ball would rebound wildly back into play and Whizzer was off again, chasing after it tirelessly.

"Any idea what the score is?" grinned Rakesh as he trotted past Worm.

"Not a clue. Who's counting?"

Worm stood back to take in the scene. The mill was alive again, both inside and out, a stark contrast to the dilapidated shell he'd viewed after breakfast in the grey morning mist. He then gazed towards the drab hostel with its dark gritstone walls and chuck-led to himself.

"At least that place hasn't changed much over the years. It's never going to win any beauty prizes."

Worm was tempted to try and sneak a proper look at the children's wretched sleeping accommodation, but he sud-denly realized that the game had come to a halt. Even time itself seemed to be standing to attention. He just caught Whizzer's warning.

"Bow down. It's the Master!"

6 Kickabout

The pauper children bowed, curtseyed and doffed their headgear to an elderly gentleman who had appeared in the corner of the yard nearest to the river. He was smartly dressed in a heavy three-piece suit and top hat, and each of the travellers felt his forceful gaze fall upon them in turn.

"I'm not bowing to him," growled Ryan. "He's not my master."

The man beckoned to them and they obeyed like lambs, despite Ryan's bravado, as if they too were under his control.

"I am Sir Samuel Vernon, Master of Mannington Mill," he announced. "And who might you be, my fine fellows? You are not from around these parts, that is clear."

"You can say that again, mate," muttered Ryan.

"You will have to speak up," the man said. "I am slightly deaf. Too much time spent in these mills, I venture."

Worm motioned to the others to let him be their spokesman. "I hope you don't mind us mixing with your young workers, sir," he began politely – and loudly. "Our parents are taking the waters at Buxton Spa for their health and have allowed us to walk the countryside today. We came upon your excellent mill by chance."

Worm's teammates looked at him in amazement, wondering how he had concocted such a story. "Just listen to him," grinned Dazza. "He's revelling in all this history lark."

"Sure sounds convincing to me," admitted Speedie. "I'd have been too tongue-tied to speak to this bloke like he's doing."

"Have you seen inside?" asked the Master, his manner softened by Worm's flattery. "The machines are the very latest in design."

"Um, yes, we did take a quick look round," answered Worm truthfully.

The man laughed. "My people probably took you young gentlemen to be factory inspectors, come to check their working conditions. I pride myself that they are looked after better than any others hereabouts."

"Even the children, sir?" asked Worm daringly.

"Of course. The inspectors would find nothing amiss in my mill. No child works more than ten hours a day."

"Ten hours?" gasped Anil.

"Used to be far more, of course.

Don't know how lucky they are. Now take these poor little blighters, for example..."

The Master turned and indicated a large group of children that had straggled up behind him from the river footpath. They were now leaning against a wall, awaiting instructions. The Rangers noticed them for the first time and were genuinely appalled by their appearance. Their rags made the Mannington children look fashion-conscious by comparison.

"They're not yours, then?" said Jacko.

"Certainly not. They are undernourished and overworked. I would not allow mine to get into that state."

"Where are they from?"

"Sterne Mill, just up the river," said the Master. "They belong to old Elias Sterne. I've persuaded him to let some of his younger folk come and join mine once a week to receive some education and recreation."

"Is this their first visit, sir?" Worm prompted.

"It is. I told him he ought to start treating his workers decent now that we have a new queen on the throne."

"Queen Victoria!" Stopper hissed to the others. "At least we know what time we're in now."

"So when did she become queen?" whispered Rakesh.

Stopper hesitated, unsure of his dates. "Er, better ask Worm later."

Worm was in full flow, eager to improve things for all the children. "We were just showing your youngsters how to play football," he told the Master. "These others could join in for a while, sir, if you wish."

"Capital!" he exclaimed. "Be good for them. You carry on."

The Master sat down on a barrel by

the wall to watch, leaving the Rangers wondering how best to begin with the nervous visitors.

"We ought to tidy up the yard a bit first," suggested Stopper. "It's dangerous with broken glass and stuff all over the place."

"Trust you to want to start caring for the environment," Jacko grinned, teasing Stopper about his newfound interest since their trip into the future.

"Come on, everybody," Dazza called out. "Litter duty. Work before play. Let's show the Master how to clean up his yard!"

The activity helped to break the ice between the groups of children as they set about the task together. It didn't take very long with so many willing hands.

"Us against them!" Whizzer suddenly cried in excitement.

He set off on a mazy dribble through a bunch of bemused boys from Sterne Mill and chipped the ball skilfully against the wall.

"GOAL!" he shrilled. "Goal!"

He danced a little jig of delight, one arm raised *à la* Ryan, before he realized that everybody was gawping at him. "What's up?" he asked, looking sheepishly about him.

"No goal," stated Jacko firmly. "We haven't started yet."

"Show him the yellow card, ref!" laughed Speedie.

"We need some proper goals this time," Dazza insisted. "The drainpipes on the walls should do for posts and I'll go in goal for Sterne, OK?"

"Poor old Sterne," Rakesh said impishly. "They've got no chance now."

The Sterne children needed a lot of help. Most of the Rangers ended up playing for them during the game to keep Whizzer and company at bay. What the Mannington side lacked in skill –

Whizzer apart – they made up for in sheer numbers and pressed home their advantage.

The Rangers often found themselves at full stretch to try and keep the score down. The goals were very wide and not even Dazza could prevent many of the shots going in.

"You won't catch me diving on this yard," he said in his own defence. "I'd break my arm. We've got another match this afternoon, I hope."

"Are we gonna be able to get back in time to play?" asked Speedie anxiously.

"Go forward in time, you mean," Dazza grinned. "Don't ask me. See what Worm says."

Worm could only shrug. "I guess we'd better start trying soon. I think we've done all we can here."

"What d'yer mean?" asked Ryan. "We haven't done anything yet, apart from have a game of footie."

"Exactly. And you've seen how much all these kids have enjoyed it. We've opened up a whole new world for them. They'll want to keep playing the game long after we've gone, I bet."

"They *will* need one thing, though, in order to do that," Stopper said.

Ryan realized what Stopper was referring to and nodded his agreement. Worm was more enthusiastic. "This ball's just perfect for them, isn't it? Won't puncture, so they can go on using it for ages."

"At least our dads won't mind us losing this one," Stopper sighed.

"Your dad might. He was wanting to take a closer look at it for some reason," Ryan reminded him, just as a whistle blew. "Hey, what's that? Full-time?"

All the players looked round to see who had the whistle. It was the Master. "Well done, everybody," he called out. "A victory for Mannington, I calculate.

Lesson time now. Line up against the wall."

Worm wasn't surprised to see that Whizzer already had the ball safely clutched in his arms. Boy and ball were clearly not to be parted.

"You're a real star," Worm told him. "You keep playing football now every chance you get, OK?"

"We will, Mister. We'll win every time."

"Got a budding Ryan there, all right," grinned Jacko. "I reckon the future of football is safe in his hands – and feet!"

7 Reunions

Sir Samuel Vernon shook each of the Rangers by the hand in farewell. "This game of football will become a regular Friday fixture," he promised.

"That's good," Worm said loudly. "It will make all the children fitter and healthier, including the ones from Sterne Mill."

Worm was satisfied that it was at least a step in the right direction. Playing football would give them something to look forward to each week, a welcome break from all the terrible hardships and drudgery of their lives. He felt it was as much as the

Rangers could hope to achieve, but he was especially glad that they'd been able to help the Sterne kids, too.

"We'd better be off now, sir," he continued. "We still have a long way to go. Would you mind if we had another look inside before we leave?"

The Master granted permission, delighted to think they were showing such an interest in his mill. For a horrible moment, the travellers feared he was even going to offer them a personal guided tour.

As they entered the factory, they were instantly hit by a wall of noise from the clunking machinery. "C'mon, let's get into that tunnel quick," yelled Anil.

The boys soon reached the spot where they had left the torches and then stepped uncertainly into the cellar. There was no brick barrier to block their path.

"So what do we do now?" Ryan demanded to know.

"No use going up into the hostel," said Rakesh. "Got no wish to share that Victorian dormitory. Besides, my toothbrush won't have arrived yet!"

"What about the chute?" said Speedie desperately. "The grille's open. That's got to be our way back, surely."

"Worth checking out," said Stopper. "Go on, Worm, nip up and have a quick shufti. This is your speciality."

There was no point in arguing. Worm allowed himself to be helped up on to the chute until his head was above the level of the grille and he could scramble out. The boys' hopes were raised when he disappeared from view, but dashed again as he loomed back over them.

"Just went to peer round the side of the hostel," he explained. "Vernon's still in the yard with all the pauper kids. He's got Whizzer next to him, demonstrating some ball skills!"

Worm slithered down the coal-blackened chute to rejoin his anxious teammates. "We've never had any trouble getting back before," said Jacko, trying to disguise his own alarm. "I mean, it's just sort of happened."

"Well, I don't fancy being stuck here," muttered Dazza. "And I'm sure not working in that mill. Given me a headache just walking through it."

As he spoke, the others realized that their heads were beginning to hurt too.

They sank to their knees as the pressure and nausea increased, closing their eyes in pain. But not before Worm saw the tunnel fading. It was slowly being covered by a wall.

"Are you lot down there?" The shout seemed to echo down the years and as they blinked open their eyes once more, they couldn't see anything at first.

"Who's that?" croaked Jacko.

"Me! Mr Thomas. Who do you think it is, Father Christmas?"

"Dad!" Ryan called out, never more relieved to hear his voice. "What are you doing here?"

"That's a stupid question. I want to know what you're all doing down there in the dark. Come out of that cellar immediately."

The boys flicked on their torches and Worm went over to touch the brick wall. "It's solid enough," he confirmed. "No good bashing your head against that now. Looks like we're safely back in the present, guys."

"Phew! Bit of a nasty moment, there," breathed Jacko. "Let's get up that chute before Time decides to play any more of its tricks on us."

"Yeah, reckon we've done more than our fair share of putting the world to rights," said Dazza. "We only came here to play football."

"I think that's what we were destined to do," said Worm meaningfully.

"Are you coming up or not?" demanded Mr Thomas.

"You'd better go first again, Ryan, and calm your dad down a bit," said Jacko. "Try and think up a good excuse why we were here."

Ryan scuttled up the chute, holding on to the chain, and grinned sheepishly as he looked over the grille. "Er, April Fool, Dad!"

"*April Fool!* Is that all you can say?"

exclaimed his dad in exasperation. "I've been searching everywhere. Thought you'd got lost."

"Same thought crossed my mind for a minute," Ryan admitted. "Nearly vanished without trace down a black hole!"

The footballers of Tanfield Rangers were treated to a light pre-match meal by their hosts, sitting at long tables in the private boarding school's oak-panelled refectory.

When the visitors' minibuses had first arrived at the school, the time travellers could scarcely believe their eyes as they read the name on the main gateway.

SIR SAMUEL VERNON COLLEGE
Boarding School for Boys –
Founded 1862

"Nobody told us we were going to be playing at the Samuel Vernon College," gasped Worm.

Mr Thomas shrugged as he drove along the tree-lined drive that wound through the school grounds. "Didn't think the name would mean anything to you. Have you actually heard of this bloke, then?"

"Er, think I've come across him somewhere," said Worm, covering his tracks. "Been learning more about life in Victorian times recently."

"You and your history!" he laughed, scrunching to a halt in the gravelled car park. "Bet you can't wait to get back home to catch up with all the reading you've missed this week."

"No substitute for real experience," said Worm enigmatically.

When the players climbed out, Worm cornered Stopper. "Why didn't you tell us your dad's old school was founded by Vernon?"

"I didn't know, did I?" Stopper defended himself. "He's always just called it the college."

A man in a flowing black gown came to meet them, greeting Mr Stoppard warmly. "Good to see you again, Stopper. Welcome back."

"Stopper?" queried Jacko to his teammate. "Was that your dad's nickname as well?"

Stopper grinned, embarrassed. "'Fraid so. Can't avoid it, I guess."

Stopper Senior was all smiles when he turned to the Rangers party. "Let me introduce an old school chum of mine, now one of the masters here himself. This is Mr Wiseman, better known to everyone as Whizzer!"

"Some of your lads look a bit shocked. Not used to hearing a teacher called by his nickname to his face," the school-master laughed. "I think they'll have had enough of us Whizzers by the end of the day, though. The latest in the line is captain of the college team!"

Worm couldn't resist interrupting. "Does that name run in your family, too, like Stopper?"

Mr Wiseman nodded. "It goes back several generations. When old Samuel Vernon set up this school, he appointed my ancestor, a former mill boy of his, as its first headmaster – 'Whizzer' Wiseman. Nice story, don't you think?"

The travellers grinned. They liked the sound of it very much indeed.

"A great man, Sir Samuel," the teacher finished. "He was a rich mill owner who gave most of his money to charities for the poor and did much to improve conditions for child-workers in local cotton mills – including playing football. A man ahead of his time, you might say."

After lunch, as the footballers began to troop out of the refectory, Ryan pulled certain teammates aside.

"What's up?" asked Dazza.

Ryan simply stepped to one side,

revealing a small show cabinet on a table behind him. He enjoyed the astonished looks on their faces.

"Couldn't take my eyes off it during the meal," he grinned. "But better not let your dad see it, Stopper."

Mounted inside the cabinet was a battered grey object with lots of bits gouged out of its pockmarked surface. But it still looked as though it would bounce.

Engraved on a gold plaque underneath the ball were the words:

The first football – origin unknown. Given to the college by Mr "Whizzer" Wiseman, Headmaster, 1862.

"Origin unknown!" Jacko laughed. "We could tell them, if they liked – not that anybody would ever believe us!"

8 They think it's all over...

The match kicked off in bright sunshine on a soggy pitch and the college captain tested out the conditions immediately. It must have been fate that pitted him in direct opposition to Worm.

Whizzer collected the ball on the left wing, took on Worm down the touchline and beat the Rangers' full-back for speed. Only the surface water in the penalty area slowed him enough for Worm to recover and make a sliding tackle, conceding a corner.

The two boys helped each other up. "See I shall have to mark you a bit closer," Worm smiled ruefully. He felt so weary, a hard game against a fast, tricky winger was the last thing he wanted. Whizzer may have been small like the mill urchin, but this one was fit and well-fed.

Stopper was clearly thinking along the same lines. After he'd headed the corner away, the centre-back grinned at his fellow defender. "Bit different from playing in that old yard, eh? Whizzer's come a long way."

"Yeah, about one and a half centuries."

"Quit rabbiting, you two, and concentrate on the game," yelled Dazza from his goal. "They look a bit useful, this lot."

The Rangers certainly struggled to keep the lively college attack in check and their prospects of winning the final match of the tour did not appear good.

The heavy pitch wasn't going to help any tired legs and Rangers had plenty of those.

They were wearing their royal blue strip with the name RANGERS printed in large white letters across their backs. Worm's shirt was already muddied up after his tackle, but at least the team's initials, T.R., embroidered on the left breast, were still clearly visible.

"Time Rangers" he liked to think they

now stood for after this week!

The Rangers managed to hold out against the red-striped college side until midway through the first half but the goal, when it came, was well worth waiting for – at least for the home supporters. It was a beauty!

Receiving a pass inside his own half, Whizzer slipped the ball through Rakesh's legs and found himself confronted by Worm again. It was no

contest. Dummying one way and then the other, he left Worm sitting in a puddle on the halfway line and sprinted for goal.

"Close him down, Stopper!" cried Dazza. "Go to him."

Jacko was trying to intercept the winger as well, but Whizzer was too quick for both of them. He outpaced Jacko and rode Stopper's late tackle superbly, leaping clear of the wild, desperate lunge. There was only the goalkeeper to beat. As Dazza raced out to narrow the shooting angle, Whizzer never even attempted to dribble round him. He simply struck the ball in his stride.

Dazza was vaguely aware of something whistling past his head. Only when he heard the swish of the netting behind him, did he realize it must have been the ball. The keeper stood near the edge of his penalty area, arms outstretched in helplessness, as Whizzer wheeled away to the touchline to receive the congratulations of his teammates.

Ryan watched enviously. He'd had little opportunity to practise his own goal celebrations. The nearest he'd come to scoring so far was when he fastened on to a loose ball after a defender had slipped, but his snapshot went into the side netting.

It was the closest in fact that the whole team came to troubling the college goalkeeper before half-time. They'd hardly been given a ghost of a chance.

Rangers had their "Player of the Season", Dazza, to thank for preventing an avalanche of goals in their own net. Time and again he came to his side's rescue with fine saves. The best of these was a swooping dive to his left to turn an awkward, skidding shot around the foot of the post.

The players trailed to the touchline at the interval, knowing what to expect.

They were right. Mr Thomas blasted them with both barrels.

"This is the worst display I've seen from you all season," he bellowed. "I've seen some bad ones, but this is a five-star stinker!"

The managers rang the changes throughout the team for the second half, bringing on all the subs. Of the travellers, Worm, Rakesh and Anil now found themselves as spectators, while Jacko moved from midfield to play next to Stopper to bolster the defence.

"Right, one last big effort," Mr Stoppard demanded. "Get stuck in. Let's see you fight your way back into this game."

For the first ten minutes, however, the story was much the same and the Rangers' new-look central defence was stretched to the limit. Stopper headed a shot off the line and Jacko hacked the ball away to safety off Whizzer's toes as the winger looked certain to score.

Only gradually did the Rangers begin to find a better blend and rhythm, aided by a strengthening wind in their favour. They used the advantage well, pinning the home side back more into their own half of the field. Even Whizzer struggled to find the space to set off on one of his dribbles.

"We're on top," Anil realized in surprise. "Wish this wind had been with us in the first half when we were playing. Hardly saw the ball."

Rakesh nodded in sympathy. "I was too busy trying to help Worm deal with that Whizzer. You can see where he gets his talents from, eh?"

"Strange how things can work out," mused Worm. "Bet they would have played rugby here rather than soccer if it hadn't been for us. We started all this."

"Sshh!" hissed Anil. "Don't tell the managers that, whatever you do. They'd probably lynch us, the mood they were in at half-time!"

Their mood now, thankfully, was a good deal better.

"Playing a bit more like we know they can," said Mr Stoppard.

"Aye, about time too," Mr Thomas replied. "But what we need now is a goal. Time's running out."

The Rangers were aware of that fact too and forced a succession of corners. Speedie took most of them, inswingers from one side and outswingers from the other, but each one was cleared, adding to Rangers' frustration.

"You go up for this next one, Stopper," said Jacko. "Your extra height might cause a bit of panic. I'll hold back and look after things here."

It was very rare for Stopper to advance as far as the opposition's penalty area. He almost felt like he needed a passport in such foreign territory. He normally didn't stray much further than the half-way line.

His arrival nearly paid dividends straight away. As the college tried to reorganize their marking to counter Stopper's threat in the air, Ryan was allowed more space. The number nine connected with Speedie's low corner on the volley, crashing it goalwards. A defender on the line did his job, although he knew nothing about the shot until the

ball struck him painfully in the stomach. It doubled him up and deflected away for yet another corner.

"Might as well stay up for this one as well," Stopper decided while the boy was allowed to regain his breath. "You never know your luck."

His luck was in. Speedie's corner this time was high and long, sailing over players' heads towards Stopper's soaring leap at the far post. He met the ball square on the forehead and sent it back across goal, wide of the keeper and underneath the crossbar.

"The equalizer!" yelled Ryan. "One all!"

Stopper was lying prone in the muddy goalmouth, mobbed and nearly suffocated beneath a pile of relieved teammates. He was in a semi-daze for the remaining few minutes of the game, but fortunately his defensive skills were not required.

The referee blew his whistle for full-time and the teams gave each other the traditional three cheers. Whizzer and Stopper also exchanged shy grins as they shook hands.

"Well played," said Whizzer generously. "You deserved a draw in the end. You'll have to come back next year for a replay."

"Maybe," Stopper smiled. "Right now, I think we've done enough travelling. We'll all be glad to get back home."

It was a surprisingly quiet return journey. The players were too tired to find the energy for more than a few snatches of football songs, but at least Mr Thomas was happy after their second-half revival. He was actually whistling as he drove along familiar roads not far from Tanfield.

"The week's gone really quick," he remarked. "Doesn't time fly when you're enjoying yourselves?"

The driver glanced round at the outburst of giggles. "What's so funny? Bet you all wish you could turn the clock back and start the tour again."

"Reckon we'd need a time machine to do that," Jacko grinned.

Ryan took up the idea with enthusiasm, if not quite in the way his dad had intended. "Hey! We *could* do it again. How about the Rangers going away somewhere in the summer holidays on a pre-season trip?"

The players liked the sound of that, but Worm was more reflective. "Yeah, but I'm sorry this tour's over now," he said sadly. "It's history!"